Jenny

My Diary

THURSDAY

Bought a lovely fuchsia print dress today. So full of brightness. Really cheers me up. I think it's more to Anthony's taste than to Gerard's. Whom would I really like to please?

SATURDAY

Smashed Susan at tennis! Superb production of LULU at the National. Peter Hall is not deteriorating with age.

Gerard brought up the question of buying into a shelter group. I hate the idea. More and more people being infected by these thoughts. Truly abhorrent. Don't think I'd even want to live after an atomic World War III. But it may cause a big row if I don't sort of go along. No point in fighting such a silly battle. Guess I feel guilty about my involvement with Anthony.

MONDAY

Wonderful! Spent the afternoon making love and drinking wine in a Pimlico hotel. Anthony makes me feel like

I'm the most bubbly, exciting, inspiring woman in the world. He admired my dress more than Gerard. Did I buy it for him?

TUESDAY

William really can't stand the school he's at. What to do? Boarding is out. I must talk to Gerard about it soon.

I think our production unit should show Bob MacDonald. His Citz Company deserves a commercial run.

Going to buy a bottle of Champagne tomorrow for Anthony. What fun!

THURSDAY

Incredible waste of money! Gerard came home and told me he had made a down-payment on a shelter near Alton. "It's well in excess of government recommendations" he said. I almost laughed. Best thing about it is that it is near Jane Austen's house at Chawton ... can't see anything else good to say about investing in an atomic age mausoleum. I could only tell Anthony about it reluctantly. His only comment was ironic : " I see : All men and women are not going to be cremated equal ."

We're going to have a look with the kids next week-end. There'll be a big barbecue American style. Is this prophetic ?

SATURDAY

Gerard made intense love to me last night. So lucky to have such a husband ...

MONDAY

Had an awful dream of insects crawling all over dead trees, as if they had nothing more to eat. They were creeping everywhere ... Gerard's tomb. The dream was in Black and White ... or rather Black ! Black ! Black !

TUESDAY

Drank rather too much Chablis at Drones yesterday afternoon. Then went out and bought a pretty red hat with a feather. Crazy thing to do. I never wear a hat, so why did I do it? Guess I hate to be predictable, even to myself.

WEDNESDAY

Joel is so committed to a big profit, he can't see Robert MacDonald. Find it depressing to wait around till the next, stale American musical.

FRIDAY

Bill wants to take up the piano. Says he's tired of his cello. Tried without success to tell him he could do both. Must go easy with him. Joel suggests I go and spend three days in Glasgow to take a look at the Citz and their new production. Christ!

SUNDAY

Too much to write. Good drive down to Worldham talking about schools. Fascinating how Bill takes after me and Simon after Gerard. Simon says he wants to be an engineer just like his Dad.

Meeting the fall-out shelter crowd was surprising. What a lot! Accountants,

computer programmers, advertising exec-
utives, a film processor, a builder, a super-
market buyer, a travel agent, even a hair
dresser. Is it some kind of cross-section of
the population? They didn't appear hyster-
ical, neurotic, or even very much like
survivors. All under forty. All with kids.
Simon and Bill rather liked some of them.
They were effusively welcoming. I guess
they're glad to have a new couple to make
up for the one that dropped out of their
little club. Yes, that's what it is, a crazy
kind of a club. Barbecue made the gather-
ing seem like a club outing.

Then the shelter! It's a concrete maze built
into a hill. Like going back to the caveman
days... except that they've tried to think of
everything: a separate generator for
electricity, big oil storage tanks, water
storage tanks, air filtration systems,
decontamination rooms...

It is all so mad. At one point I wanted

to scream about the insanity of it all. But I was also curious. Couldn't some of that energy have gone into fighting for peace... no. Working for peace? The two concrete "cave" rooms we mortgaged ourselves into for £8,000 ... each measures about 150 square feet, all equipped with wall-to-wall carpet, plug for T.V., power outlets, and light fixtures. We have to bring the rest of it in! No paint nor plaster on the walls. Gerard said he'd let me redecorate. No thanks. He doesn't know it, but he's going to have to wait a long time before he gets me back there again.

MONDAY

Talked at length to Anthony about the excursion to Worldham. Thought he would scoff at the idea. Surprised again. He thinks there may be a war as well; that I have to think about my kids. Men are amazingly alike. Thought he would talk about my surviving without him! I feel hurt he

didn't bring that up. What strange differ-
ences in sentiment between men and women.

TUESDAY

Gerard talked to me in bed last night about
international tension. After the news of the
Middle East I wondered what could get worse?
I understand nothing of big power relation-
ships except that they're always deteriorating.
What a prelude to making love!

WEDNESDAY

Bland dinner party with the Barehams
whom we met at the barbecue. Everything a
snore until they started to talk about the
shelter. The damned thing won't let up.
"They've agreed" that they'll shoot anyone
who tries to break in if and when the crunch
really comes! "They even bought a shot gun.
Ray, the petrol station owner, will man it.
Incredible! He's even had it licensed.
Start a new life, survive by shooting down

the others!

Thank God this also upset Gerard. He said we must have a meeting about it.

THURSDAY

House was burgled this afternoon. Just took the T.V. and the silver. Broke in through the kitchen door. It's all become so ritualized. The insurance company will cover it. We'll get a new T.V. and new silver. The insurance rates will go up. Then there'll be a new break-in . . .

Simon seems the most upset about it all.

I had two glasses of wine and spent an hour looking for what might be missing.

FRIDAY

Bought Anthony the most wonderful moss-green cashmere sweater. Always surprised how pleasant it is to buy a beautiful present. I anticipate the pleasure it will give.

Talked to Anthony about the shelter. He quoted Wilde : The basis of optimism is sheer terror.

SATURDAY

After the dinner with the Barthams, Gerard persuaded me to go down to Worldham again to discuss the machine gun and entry question. I'm going to stir up troubles. It's absolutely immoral... even · if the world is about to blow itself up. Strange how Gerard and I have such different opinions about survival when we've been married for 15 years.

Gerard casually mentioned that someone wanted to buy our shares for £12,000. Panic must really be setting in .

SUNDAY

What publicity ! I refused to pose for the Sunday papers in front of the

shelter. The MIRROR covered the debate
about "shutting the gates". The steel blast
doors will be shut and will remain shut
when the radiation level on the outside
monitor reads X. Nothing will open the
doors again until the safety level has
been reached ... not even if we all
die inside. It is truly incredible!
Technology at its most demonic!

MONDAY

Joel saw the story in the papers today and
all the pictures of the stock rooms filled
with food for 50 children and adults for
12 months! He asked me whether I'd let
him in? I told him women had a difficult
time keeping men out of anything. He
didn't catch that. Must be very preoccupied.
My problem is what is going to happen if
Gerard is going to drag me down? And

he'll have to drag or drug me.

TUESDAY

Can't focus on the budget problems at the office at all. Everyone huddled about the T.V. set today. The continuing Middle East crisis. Chilling. It's all building up like a nightmare. I kept on nibbling at Japanese rice crackers and rolling my own cigs. Nothing, but nothing seems to be going right. Never did understand all those explanations about a mass going critical in physics ... but that seems to be what is happening.

Called Anthony, but couldn't get through. Where is he?

WEDNESDAY

Wanted to go to the hairdresser before work today, but early – before breakfast – Gerard told me to keep the kids home. He took the train and tube to Metal Box. Too risky to go by car, he said. All incredibly upsetting. Everyone continually glued to T.V. and the radio. He called from work at 10.30 and told me to start packing the Volvo. The P.M. issued a national emergency declaration... the U.K. might be at war in a few hours. Are these the final words I'll write? Got to pack right now... Thank God Bill and Simon are home...

SUNDAY? MONDAY?

How can I write like a sane person about the horrific last three days? Words are so inappropriate, so totally inadequate. I must not let go of my sanity. Writing is a small release.

Gerard called me Wednesday and told me to drive the kids to Wordham immediately. I could hear in his voice that he would tolerate no argument. He was going to get there by train. I wanted to come home first. He said every minute was crucial. There was panic in the streets. All routes out of London were closed because of the National Emergency. Only trains could go out. But it would

be possible for me to drive from Guildford
with Simon and Bill.

The scenes on the road were incredible ...
the panic and fright on people's faces was
unbelievable. Bill and Simon looked
pale and hardly spoke. We listened to
the radio.

Arrived at the shelter at about 1.30. Pryce
was guarding the entrance with the
shotgun. He bade us welcome and told us
to unload the Volvo before parking it
at some distance away. Ronald
Trakin and Lester Pinder helped to get
it all out.

There was nothing in our "apart-
ment" except what we had brought in
the Volvo and the sleeping bags. Everyone was watching the T.V. set in the
communal dining room.

The Prime Minister declared war
at 3 p.m. Ten minutes later missiles
were falling all over England and the T.V.

reception stopped. Nobody knows what blast waves rocked this island. We didn't feel much at all. Two families apparently tried to make their way into the shelter, but Pryce shot them in cold blood. He was terribly upset. I think he has suffered a nervous breakdown.

I wanted to get out, but Trakin argued that I had to stay for the children. I didn't want to be trapped in a tomb without my husband. Don't know what happened after that, but I guess I became violent and someone (Trakin?) just knocked me out.

Woke up to the cries of the children: "We're locked in and Daddy's outside." The ultimate of stupid ironies.

— floating in front of my eyes — ... during ... and particles of dust)

Time has stopped. There are no more days or nights in this hide-out. My life seems over... and yet here I am alive with my two boys. There is No Way Gerard could come in now...

I'm not alone in this mess. Jim Groves couldn't make it. Neither could the Barehams nor the Munros and their children. Angela Rowan also was locked out with her kids. Wilson, her husband, has been trying to help William and Simon We moved into the rooms of the Munros. They were all supplied for the emergency. Beds are better than sleeping bags on the hard floor. The kids are very upset They're in some state of shock. The T.V.'s stopped transmitting... They feel cut

off from the world, from reality:
Their reality. And mine?
I want to write and write and
WRITE to drown out the misery.

I can't sleep... When I doze off
briefly the nightmares are so
horrible I wake up. And when I
look around and realize where I am,
what has happened to me, the
living nightmare seems even
worse.

TUESDAY?

None of us
knows anything. The
electro-magnetic shock
waves appear to have
damaged our radio. The
war may be at an end or
a standstill. There have

been no more blasts. But what is left
and how? We don't know. The
geiger-counter on the outside reads
high danger. 800 rads. It may be,
of course, that it is covered in
radioactive dust. Only when there
are rains will the dust wash away
and tell us the truth: will the
doors ever open again?

Tuesday again. We had a group
meeting and Trakin pushed through
a "No Smoking" measure. He really
has a dictatorial streak in him.
I had been rolling my own, but it does
smell up the place and the air conditioning
is weak. The air we breathe is so stale.

We won't last long at this rate, he
cautioned. But does it matter at
all? How long will it last in this
lead-lined, concrete tomb?

WEDNESDAY

The 40 watt bulbs are flickering
~~badly~~ dimly. Our generator unit
has little power. I am flickering too.
ONE WEEK since we entered the
shelter. Seven days. From now on
the days will have no more
significance. I will number
them. This is day 7.

"We" decide to hold a religious
service. So I am part of "we" now?
There is no one to officiate, so we all
pray silently in our own way.

Could a God exist in a world where this can happen? If there is a supreme divinity, there must be a touch of sadism in "its" psychological make up.

The sound of voices seems so different down here. I feel people have trouble getting the words out. I keep on hearing strained vocal chords and lisps and stammers.

8

The ceilings are so low I feel claustrophobic. The raw, unfinished texture of the concrete is a constant reminder of where I am, how I am.

Bill and Simon are to take classes every day in two rooms which used to "belong" to us. I'm doing Shakespeare with the older ones. We don't have enough books, so I have to read. MIDSUMMER NIGHT'S DREAM. Don't know why I chose it? Something light, I guess.

9

The children are desperately trying to adjust. It is in their nature. Bill has got a girl friend Helen Groves. She's 14 and her father got locked out like Gerard... Gerard. my poor Gerard. and Anthony ???

I think I'll scream. There, that's
better. Got to get a grip on my incipient
madness.

Simon looks all bleary-eyed, my
little angel. There are about four
matys of his age. The fact that they
are not alone, that they have a little
gang seems to help him. By contrast,
I feel totally bereft. None of these people
not even Rowan Wilson who has been
so good to us, means anything to me.
They are like Zombies. Why bother
to describe them? Their existence
isn't relevant to my past...it seems
even less pertinent as to how I'm
feeling right now. Nothing in a
    sense seems real.

Always imagined there would be some contact with the outside world in this shelter. But the planners made sure there would be none. Not even rats can burrow their way in.

The maniacs thought they had covered all contingencies... but they forgot to include decontamination suits. It might have been possible to walk around in a space suit... or even a diver's rubber suit. Probably would have cost too much money. And then there was the question of that door. I cannot believe that I am entombed down here and

that everyone else is dead above!
Or if not dead,
they're dying. And
how many others
in england and
America and
Russia are
trapped
like I am?
I recall that
big project in the
limestone quarries
near Bath. There
must be hundreds
down there. But
what is
the
point
of it ???

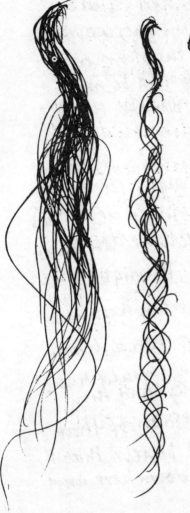

11 Thought about Anthony in last
night's sleep period (That's
what Trakin has decided
         upon. Sleep periods
                when the
         lights are dimmed and
      the temperature goes down
two or three degrees.) I wish
that I could have died in
Anthony's arms... or in
Gerard's ... I still can't believe
that I'm trapped alive down here.
It can't be true. It can't be real.

Must try to keep up my spirits
         for Simon and Bill.

12 The food in limbo is deadly. So the children tell me. I have no taste. I eat as if by rote because I'm told. It is all made up from reconstituted types of dried food and tins. They are putting together a "fall-out shelter recipe book!"

Bill is learning how to program a computer. I thought he would want to smash any such damn thing. But he has no bitter feelings at all about the means to this end...

13 Extraordinary how much kindness there is down here. I would not have thought such concern possible. Does it merely mask our weakness?

Cicely Pinder chatted with me a few hours ago. She's having an affair with David Herbert and his wife is having an affair with John Martin and... I lost all count and interest, how can they carry on like that? As if this shelter were some kind of suburban swap-club?

Cicely is a gossip. She said that there were more women than men in our group of 17 adults and 23 children and that this was bound to create trouble when we regained interest... interest..? Am I crazy?

Some muddled thoughts: It's not promiscuity, it is bottomless despair — the haunting, screaming emptiness that follows prolonged, intense fear. How is one to react to being buried alive?

I think they are merely reaffirming
or pathetically trying to reaffirm
their underground humanity.
It is like a stream.

14

Read Act II of MIDSUMMER NIGHT
to the class today. Scenes from
another planet. Another civilization?
Obviously ours cannot continue

And another meeting. They seem
to be getting more frequent...
Trakin said that showers had to be
kept to a minimum. There is a strain
on the filtration systems which
means we must be more careful
with the use of water. Similarly
there is a problem of washing
dishes and washing our clothes.

We're simply going to have to get used to a lot of smells!

Confess that I didn't notice anything until people started talking about smells. Have I been anaesthetized? Insensible to most things. I look at my fingers: five fingers ... one hand.

15   Nightmares upon nightmares.

Last doze I dreamed of Gerard. He was trying to get into the shelter, pounding on the doors .. but no reply ... I only heard the pounding in my head, in my heart.

Watched some old cassettes today.
Today? I have no idea any more
what turn of the clock it is.
Whether it is Sunday or Thursday.
Only the numbers count. Everybody
else seems to have lost interest as
well. We're settling down for a long
pull.

Strange what they brought down with
them from the old civilization! Of
course they were unprepared to
take what really mattered. Three
taped episodes from DALLAS! It's
enough to note what incredibly
poor actors they all were. I wonder
what is left of Texas? Left
in Texas? That is one civilization,
can I call it that, which no-one

will weep for.

Tried to recall the books which
had most influenced me,
which I loved best. They're
really all from my youth.

17

Can't sleep. Try to read. I can't
focus on the page. It seems
        irrelevant what the
subject is: Every word
screams at me: IT
DOESN'T MATTER.

Looked at myself in the mirror
today. I'm getting pale. Somebody

brought along an ultra-violet lamp
and we are each to sit in turn for
five minutes a day. Nevertheless we
have the pallor of long-term
prisoners.

18.

Walked around a while ago and
found everybody was playing end-
lessly at cards, as in the 18th century.
Or is it out of Beckett? I can't
bear the mindlessness of it all.

The Herberts' cat, Kappy, keeps on
brushing its orange-marmalade fur
against my legs. Why does it prefer me?

19 Wanted a good glass of wine. At
least it's something that I wanted.
That and sleep. I can't face thinking
and I can't bear my insomnia.

After "supper" tonight there was a discussion led by Wilson on our chances for survival. At the rate we were eating, suggested Trakin, we could remain underground another 11 months. Would the doors open by then?

Strange, I had the feeling some members didn't really care. They appear to be settling down to the routines of this limbo. And some actually may be enjoying the drama of it, despite the incredible sterility. Eleven months? It seems as inconceivable to me as 6 million Jews killed, 100 Megaton Hydrogen bombs falling, or Britain's former National Debt. I guess that's ...

I wish I could breathe. The air is stale and musty. Some heavily filtered air is pumped in from a nearby concrete chamber. How strange to crave for a breath of real fresh air.

I'm not finding the company human. Can't relate to the others. Only to Bill and Simon. I guess that's not entirely true. I find Trakin more and more objectionable. He is bossy and authoritarian and that masks his weak, nasty nature. But then the others are weak too. And I am weak. Oh, so frail! So on the edge.

I keep on seeing orange dots in front of me. Wonder what causes them?

Trakin said at a meeting today that we must cut down on the use of toilet paper. It won't hold out at the rate we're using it. Christ! I felt like flushing all of it. What the hell is the point of this bizarre captivity? I do not believe that life can be lived under such perverted conditions.

Thought a lot about Anne Frank. She too had to cope with incomprehensible madness. But she lived under almost normal external conditions. She breathed fresh air and saw the light. Technology was still so primitive then in her attic.

Feel such an overwhelming
   tiredness.

22
   Heather made a pass at me today.
   Blonde, distraught Heather.
   What an incredible isolation she
   feels. But isn't it overcoming
   everyone in the cave? I don't
   really fancy another human...
   but she seemed so infinitely,
   cosmically sad. I just hugged
   her and put it off ... a
   close embrace seemed to suffice.
   I can't see why she chose me?
   What have I got to offer? I
   am no less bereft than she is.
   All I know is that two negatives
   cannot make a plus.

23

I don't think the numbers
correspond to days any more.
Somebody told me that
tomorrow we'll have passed a whole
month in this limbo of the concrete
shelter. Where am I? Who am I
now? What is left of me?
I have not the flesh nor the will
of a St. Augustine

24

A month? No, it seems like an
eternity. Trakin decreed today
that we must all participate in
the keep fit classes. He's right
that we're getting flabby. I
hate this feeling that there must
be a leader... The human
species were simply too defective to

survive. That is the inevitable
conclusion that one must draw.

25

Noticed how incredibly much
sorrow there is around me;
had been
oblivious to
Pamela and
Rowan's misery
until now. Almost
completely self-absorbed.
I must try to draw,
or at least to
doodle more,
to get some feeling
back. I think at
first I'm just going
to have to fake it.

26 Spent the time doodling. Several
cave dwellers obviously think I've
gone round the bend. They don't
understand that it is a step
forward to release, towards the
dreadful reality.

Kappy keeps on visiting me. Why
can I relate better to her than to
most humans?

27. Heather gave me a haircut
today. She's adapted well to the
role of community barber.
Never cut hair in her life
before. It makes her feel more
useful.

I miss good music. There are only
a few records here. People brought
their discards and left the

best at home. No music on
the tapes except punk and
rock 'n roll. Will Mozart or
Beethoven survive for Simon
and Bill? What will they know
about art? Theatre? No. For
them it is all immaterial.
They will face the grimmest
most dreadful battle for mere
survival if they/we ever get
out.

28

Curious how the children are
forming into gangs. There are
9 kids over 11 years of age who
have joined into two cliques.
Then there are the middle
ones and the youngest. For

them a year or two is so terribly
important... and for me? What
still matters? Bill and Simon,
I guess, and they are drifting
away... their self protective
systems at work.

29

Moulds are suddenly appearing
everywhere. We noticed it
a few cycles ago, but nobody
said a word. Ugly green
blobs. Then Trakin brought it
up at dinner. At least he faces
up to things. He suggests we put
some anti-bacterial foot powder
at the entrance of the air-conditioning
vents. What if we developed
"Legionnaire's disease?" Some joke.

I long to feel a twitch, any twitch,
to prove to myself that I am alive!

30

Feel I have no invisible means
of support down here. Atheism
is not much comfort to the dying.
At least St. Thomas Aquinas
could think of limbo if he didn't
see himself making either
heaven or hell. And here I
have to live in this indefinite

suspension without the hope
of any different prospects. to
sustain me.

31 Sex in this cycle with Rowan. It
felt surprisingly good to feel
another human body. Just
did it to prove to myself I am
still alive. Does it really make
any difference? Poor, bereft
Rowan just wants warmth.
His Angela was locked out with
the two children ... she had been
trying to pick them up at boarding
school. Rowan cried later. He
misses her a lot. Feels guilty.
about surviving. We had a
secret scotch afterwards. Alcohol
is getting scarce.

32 Was told it is now two months:
60 days. I think the kids are bored
out of their minds down here. They

need to run, play, be in the fresh air. There is a rebellious feeling in Bill. He seems to resent that the adults are keeping him artificially busy all the time. What's the alternative?

My turn to cook pasta today. I hate it. The only part of the kitchen I enjoy is baking bread. Thank God they installed a good exhaust system!

33

Must be more self assertive. Get back a token of my old self. Either I must live as best I can, even in this underground hell, or I must end it bravely.

I am going to arrange theatrical shows for the children and the adults.

The children will do YOU'RE A GOOD
MAN CHARLIE BROWN. The adults
will try something harder: No. I've
got to give them something light
and silly, like HELLO, DOLLY! Yes,
I believe they've got a tape of it here
somewhere.

34

First rehearsal today for DOLLY. Funny,
I forgot to make an entry "yesterday"
about the casting. Anyway, it doesn't
matter. It's all so silly. Heather is
playing Dolly Levi. Trakin is
Horace. Eric is Cornelius.

Became more aware than ever that
we're all zombies: We are the
stalking dead. And now we're
even singing HELLO, DOLLY! The
bubbles of Carol Channing...

how remote that seems.

35

Heather came into my bed last sleep cycle. Better than having nightmares. At least I slept! Strange. the comfort of another body. I was surprised that there was nothing new, exciting or even illicit about it. No passion... Just a feeling of less loneliness. Perhaps we are past passion?

36

The kids' play is coming along quite well! Simon is playing Snoopy. He likes it. They're far more flexible than the adults. Most of the Dolly cast is simply wooden. Only Eric seems to have any flair. I guess it's because he's Jewish.

I did think of him in a physical
way after the play yesterday. What
would you have me do, Gerard?
Anthony? Mum? Dad? God?
No, there is no one.

37

Susan Trakin is very sick. Nobody
can figure out what is wrong
with her. There is no doctor here.
She is suffering from bad chills.
  Ronald is becoming tougher,
more determined than ever. He
was impossible in the rehearsal.
Couldn't force myself to correct
him : he might crack.

38

Wilson told me he came upon
Steve, Helen, Sarah, Duncan and
my Will having an orgy in the

store room. He simply closed the
door. Seemed no point in telling
them off. What have they got
left? Guess I would have done
the same. Morality in a fall-
out shelter is a dadaist joke.

39

Susan Trakin died a few
hours ago. There can be no
burial, so we slid her into
a black polythene bag and
tied the end up. Horrid.
She was a Catholic, but
there is no priest. Ronald and
the children were crying,
disconsolate. There is no
solace to be found in this shelter.

40 Another dreadful nightmare:
This time I was at a party with
Anthony. It was a beautiful summer's
eve. Everyone was eating, drinking, kissing.
I was wearing my lovely print dress ...
which I never wore. Then
suddenly one
man collapsed.
Gerard?
Then another.
Then someone
shouted
"Botulism!"
We all started
to turn
green and
throw up.
I got
violently
ill.

Woke up with
stomach spasms.

41

Heather told me she spent the
night with Ronald, but that
Pamela is after him as well.
Shall we end up clawing over the
men like bitches in season?
What a stinking, putrid lot
we are.

42

The play's the thing. But
there's a feeling of total
futility. Everybody's truly
worried sick: Physically and
literally. Cicely and Janis
keep on forgetting their
lines. Trakin can't pronounce
them at all, but I think he'll
pull himself together in a

few cycles. Eric makes the others look
worse by his professionalism. I
   kissed Eric afterwards by way
of thanks. Carol saw me. Does it
matter? Eric is very special. His
face is sad and whimsical, as if
   humour could overcome all the
horrors of this world.

43
   We've been rehearsing DOLLY
   for two weeks. What vacuity!
   It has distracted everyone. I
   never liked these empty
   American musicals: " I'm
   beginning to hate them now.
   Every note is like a grease
   stain on the concrete floor.

44 Opening night! Neither Day
nor Night nor Openings, openings,
open shall ever grace this
            shelter. Our clothes
are beginning to look shoddy.
We must save water and there
is little chance to use the
    washing machine. So it
was an opening night
without elegance. What did
it have?

The children applauding They
adored seeing their parents
perform That alone made it
worthwhile. I kept on looking
at Bill's face, and thought of
Gerard...

Afterwards, Simon presented

me with a paper flower on stage.
I cried ... when will I see a real
flower again?

45.

Had a long talk last cycle, or was
it the cycle before, about what it
must have been like in Auschwitz.
It brought me closer yet to Eric. To
the Jewish victims in the camps, the
world was incomprehensibly sadistic.
Their captors were madmen, released
from insane asylums, who were
now permitted to exercise their
dementia upon the living. Eric
said that one could not expect
to find any link with rationality
in such an environment. We
have no captors but ourselves,

On the other hand. Our environment is totally rational and yet the scope of the disaster is so overwhelming that we cannot encompass it. We simply cannot accept our fate as survivors. I am a survivor? Am I? Am? I?

Talking brought me closer yet to Eric. I think Carol is rather upset at the way I'm gravitating towards him. Well, all I have to offer is my sick spirit and my mouldy body. It isn't much.

46 I spent much time rehearsing CHARLIE BROWN. The kids are smashing. We're going to have a lot of flickering lights to make it seem like a motion

picture. I keep on wanting to cuddle
my own little Snoopy, Simon. Well,
the adults will love it tomorrow...
and then what?

Tried to elicit what Eric was like as
a little boy. Couldn't formulate a
clear picture. Eric said people are
beginning to live in this labyrinth
through their reminiscences.

47
Everyone was really turned on by
the kids. Such a spirited performance!
Afterwards we had brownies and
chocolate and there was dancing. I
danced three times with Eric. Gravity
pulls me... a restlessness which
masks the impatience of a prisoner.

48
I told Eric I wanted him to come to

me. He said he couldn't. Things were difficult enough for Carol on her own. I could see he wanted to but couldn't. Why be coy? I went to Carol and told her I was lonely, I needed company; I liked Eric. I didn't want to hurt her.

What could we do?
She said simply:
"Just join us
tonight. I don't
want to be alone."

Three's better than
one. And that's it.
Carol was very
supportive, under-
standing. God,
what a place
to be exploring
human
relationships.
Why am I acting this way? I think

it is a desperate desire to assert
life !
⸻

49

Eric read to me from Genesis : "As
the sun rose upon the earth... the
Lord rained upon Sodom and
Gomorrah sulphurous fire... He
annihilated those cities and the
entire plain and all the inhabitants
of the cities and the vegetation
of the ground..."

Eric and I are spending long
sessions discussing suffering,
existence, posterity, civilization,
the possibility of a plurality
of Gods... Ultimately we always
wind up bewildered : What was
the point of creation if it ends

in such a nuclear holocaust?
We are in agreement that we
cannot take life seriously because
it is impossible to get out of it
alive... How feeble it all is!

Is our fate ultimately that different
from the others who died in the
first minutes?

50

William is moving further away
from me. I don't think it has
anything to do with Eric and
Carol. He is finding his pleasures
and his reality with his peer group.
They don't trust those who have
led them into this predicament.
I think he and Ros Pryce are
head over heels in love. So much

the better for them. I told him I
thought Ros was a splendid girl
and that I hoped they could find
some happiness in each other's
company. He merely blushed.

51. John Martin had a fight with
Trakin. Truly horrid. They started
with fists and ended up bashing
each other with chairs... or so
said Cicely. John must have boiled
over. Trakin's petty dictatorship is
unbearable. He's such a small,
tragically small, man. Why does
he have to impose his will? Is it
in the nature of the beast or,
perhaps, is it because the rest of
us are sick sheep?

52. Big cheer this cycle; The radiation level outside has fallen
substantially. Everyone is excited,

talking about the milirads per hour!
Could it have been a big rain or a
snowfall outside? It now looks as
if the doors could open again. A
month? Two months? We all
speculate about it. What will it
be like outside? It will be spring
but will there be leaves on the
trees? or flowers? And how will
we contact others? Trakin has
already begun to plan for organized
search parties as far away as
Guildford.

Wonderful to see how the faces
brightened today. Some didn't
flicker at all, however. Like Ray
Price. He's never come out of
shock.

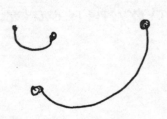

Abe Blum and Bill are becoming
close friends. Eric and I talk about
it. It pleases us. Carol, on the other
hand, seems to be retreating into
herself. She told me she is worried
about what will happen when we
get out. The underground standards
of right and wrong, of the possible
and the impossible, may not apply
above ground. The three of us
discussed this, although I feel
incapable of projecting that
long into the future. Most of
me is dead ... strange how
Carol confides in me more and
more. Brings me closer to her. I
still cannot confide in anyone
here. Are my fears too great?
Thoreau said we must not simply

be good, we must be good for something. But for what and when?

What, indeed, has happened to our
standards, to our morals during
this prolonged confinement? We've
been here months and months.
I'm not the same person I was
when I started this diary. I am
flabby, sallow-faced, grey-haired
on the outside. And inside?
I seem to have grown immune
to criticism, even to self-criticism.
My feelings and passions have
been dulled to the point where
they no longer have a cutting
edge. I am dulled and dull and
dulling.
The only goal of this self-inflicted

torture has been survival. This means
focusing on self. self. self. This is
truly the ME shelter.

And tomorrow? I know there will
never be time for trivialities again,
like pretty dresses, or hats, or parties...
and yet everything seems so impossibly
trivial and meaningless.

55

The radiation levels continue to fall.
We celebrated today by burning a
single candle to mark this incredible half year. And what will the
next six months bring? Jeremiah!
I might even get Eric's child. What
a thought ... but I am running
out of the pill. So is everyone else.
Our artificial, womb-like protection

from the outside world is coming
to an end. No matter how horrible
it will be outside, I am glad.

Talked at length to Eric and Carol
about how we might no longer be
alive if everyone had been able to
make it to the shelter. Thirteen
adults and children were kept
out. Why am I alive and my
  Gerard dead ??? Eric brought
up the notions of guilt and
suffering. His outlook is very
Jewish: philosophy tempered
by the volatility of emotions.

56
The radiation level is almost
at the exit mark. We all agree
that we should proceed most

cautiously. The survey meter we have is out of action: the batteries have gone dead. We have no batteries which work. How to test for contamination? We still have dosimeters, but they only measure the dose you have received, not the one you are about to receive. Some areas may be far more radioactive than others. The kids want to be the first to go on a search party to Alton. Eric, Carol and I wonder whether we will be able to stop them, or whether we should even try?

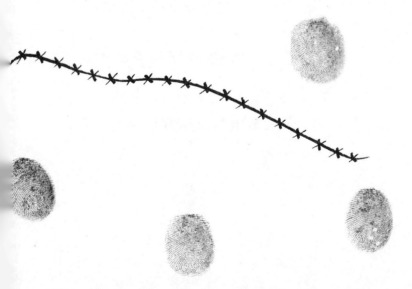

57 The ten most heard wishes over the
past months have been :

"I wish we could breathe some
                    fresh air."

"I wish we could see the sun ...
        get some sunshine."

"I wish I could see the world outside"

"I wish we could have some real meat."

"I wish we could have a bath."

"I wish we could have some fresh
                        fruit."

"I wish we could have a coke."
            (the kids)

"I wish we could smoke again."

"I wish I could have a beer...
        wine ... scotch ..."

"I wish we had colour T.V."

SUNDAY

I'm told it's not... but it does not
matter. This was the new day we had
all been waiting for so desperately.
The doors opened and nearly all of us
rushed right out, just to get a look at
the world again. I didn't really care
whether I got radiation sickness or
not... but it was horrible.

The first thing we saw after the
sun and the sky were the bones
and the torn clothes of those who
had been shot trying to enter!
What a welcome. I had forgotten
all about them. How could I ???

The next thing I noticed together
with Bill and Simon, was our

Volvo. There was a skeleton in it!
Must have been Gerard. Totally
unrecognizable... The nightmare
of nightmares come true. He
must have died there on the
outside, waiting for us. There
was nothing to do...

The sun was shining... a spring
day... and yet things were very
strange. There were no birds. Indeed
very few of the trees and scrubs had
any leaves... they all looked as if
burned or scorched. Horrid.
And then we noticed insects
everywhere: swarms of them...
beetles and bugs of all kinds.

Still, the main thing was to
    BREATHE. It was calm. No

wind. No DUST. We all put on our heaviest soles and covered our feet with polythene bags so that we wouldn't bring the radioactive dust or dirt back in. Trakin had insisted on that.

When I first went out I really had wanted to kiss the earth, in thanks, like a Pope. But when the moment came, the earth seemed strangely detestable. I can't describe it, but it was a profoundly chilling sensation. Everybody spent hours just standing about, looking at everything, touching nothing. We were not quite sure what to do next. The clouds built up and it started to rain. Many of us just stood there, just looking up. Some of the little ones took their clothes off. I loved it. I hugged Eric and Carol and

Bill and Simon. Little Simon said he hardly remembered rain.

I was happy to experience the elements again, no matter what happens after this. Not even the skeletal bones detracted from that delight. As the rain got heavier, I came back through the decontamination chamber into this hateable concrete shelter. Yes, I do hate it ... I can't stand it . . . but I knew nowhere else was safe and I didn't want to go into the car. I stayed away from it ...

The kids have decided to walk to Alton tomorrow. Several of the others tried to start their cars, but the batteries have gone dead and the roads may be impassable in any case.

I don't think I'd be up to a long walk.
Much weaker than I thought I'd be.
Just looking up at the hill where King
John had once had his hunting lodge
seemed exhausting!

TUESDAY

I waved goodbye to Will and Abe and
the little group of teenagers as they
went off to Alton with Rowan and John.
Simon stayed behind with Ann, Eric,
Carol and most of the adults. We just
sat outside, awaiting their return.

They came back towards sunset on
bicycles found in town. They were
exhausted and full of news: There
was no-one alive in Alton. The
town was full of hideous rats.
There were the bones of corpses all

around. The Police Station, an almost new building, looked as if it had been attached ... but by whom? The Co-op was open and the shelves were full of tins. They brought back lots of canned salmon, canned ham and tinned fruits ... as well as liquor.

At the feast we held outside, everyone told what they had seen, but there was no ground for optimism. We decided the first thing to do was to try and get batteries for the geiger counter: It was crucial to find out what was radioactive and what wasn't ...

WEDNESDAY

Food is going to be a big problem. We are going to be scavengers on the old food supply... and then what? What is going to grow? There are so many insects about it wouldn't make sense to plant anything outside of a greenhouse. Trakin explained to us that one could grow much more in those than one might imagine.

I had a long talk with Eric and Carol today about why we are alive? We walked up past the footpath up to the Three Horseshoes. Hot & Cold snacks the sign read. "The Potter's Shop"... We took some beers out of the pub. Why were we alive? Why us? Why me? What the hell is the point? Carol seemed almost as negative as I appeared to be. Eric is more of a fatalist. I simply must not let the incredibly black side of all this overwhelm me.

THURSDAY

John and Herb got the Rover going

and drove to Petersfield. There were
fallen branches and trees everywhere
and there were broken down vehicles
as well. They made it to another
shelter John knew about. He opened
the doors and there was a terrible
stench! All inside had died.

No batteries were found, but it appeared that several of the stores in
Petersfield had recently been looted -
maybe a month ago or so, Herb
guessed. There was little food there.
At least this meant that somewhere
there were survivors like us. But
Where?

What next? A trip to Guildford?
It seemed risky. It was likely that the
bases at Farnham, Aldershot and

Odiham all had been hit. None of us really has any clear idea what to do, but we agreed it was risky to go East. Trakin demanded, in his own bossy way, that we stick together. That is probably a sufficient motive for me to go my own way. We debated for some time the idea of going down to the sea and taking a few boats to sail to warmer and less contaminated climates ... but exactly where?

FRIDAY

Several of the kids who had gone to Alton are suffering from nausea. I think it must be a form of radiation sickness. At least it is not contagious. John and Herbert, who got a greater dose of exposure than the rest of us, are also feeling sick. There is little we can do to prevent them from

throwing up. Fortunately, Will seems
to be relatively OK.

SUNDAY

Eric, Carol and I talked about moving
to a house in Chawton. There is no
reason to stay in this shelter any longer.
It is driving us all claustrophobic, crazy.
We cycled to Chawton, through Alton.
An incredible two hour journey. No
ghost towns were ever as eerie as this.

Chawton itself only has the little Post
Office/store and the house of Jane
Austen. It is impossible to live in her
house. The place is a museum and the
exhibits reminded me only of death....
I hate unlived in houses. I took some
cigarettes out of the machine at the
Greyfriar pub across the street.

Chawton House itself is a wonderful

16th century, three storey mansion with few modern conveniences ... The exterior is a mixture of flint stone and red brick. The wings are in mellow red brick and the long leaded windows let in the light. It is a house full of history and thus particularly appealing ... after being cut off from the past in this shelter. Am I beginning to repeat myself down here?

The children are still sick, but I think they are getting a bit better. At least they have stopped throwing up.

MONDAY

I discussed Chawton with Bill and Simon. Bill says he, Steve, Helen, Ros, Sarah and Duncan have decided to cycle together towards the West. They have talked it over at length. There is going to be a premium on food and

there is no way we can survive if we
stick together. Survival, argues Bill,
is the only objective left.

I can already see them roaming as a
pack... Why does that make me upset?
Basically, I agree with their thoughts
I know I have no strength to stop them.
I suggest that they go to Cornwall and
that if things don't work out there,
fishing, and so forth, that they then
take a boat and head south...

They plan to go tomorrow. I can only
wish them luck. I explained I would
leave a note on the Post Office door
at Chawton should I move... or should
they come back. I asked that Bill
also leave a note on the Post Office
door at St. Ives.

At night we all drank a lot of the

now plentiful plonk. I think Bill got
high for the first time. Only such a little
boy to be going on his own. It is terrible...
all terrible.

WEDNESDAY

I cried and cried as we waved goodbye
to the brave kids. My Bill! Gone forever
it seems. What a world he has to inherit!
I was surprised I could still cry so much
after all of this. Carol and Eric joined
me in the tears...

How could I have let my Bill. my only
Bill. go? How could I? It is monstrous...
What is there but the wailing and the
gnashing of teeth.

THURSDAY

Today we moved to Chawton. At last
we're out of the HOLE. The welcoming sign inscribed over the door at
Chawton: "Suivant Saint Pierre"
("following Saint Peter"). I love the

large green Cedar tree and the Yew...
They are relatively unaffected by
the radioactivity. The Boxwoods don't
seem to have survived quite as well.
There is a blight on many of the leaves.

Tonight I will sleep in an 18th century
bed. I took some fresh sheets out of the
cupboard. Simon comes back to tell me
of all sorts of surprises... Perhaps we
shall be able to plant seeds in the
greenhouses around here? I long for
fresh vegetables.

FRIDAY
Heather. Rowan and Diana have
decided to live near us as well. It's
going to be very tough surviving
for a long time off the Key Market
in Alton. We've tried to take out all
the rice, flour and staples which

we could. Fortunately there are a lot of stores and houses in the area and each house has its provisions.

We also got lots of rat poison and have scattered it around the house here. That should get rid of the beasts quickly. It is strange that there are no pets any more: we took dogs and cats so much for granted. I miss Kappy since she went off with the Herberts.

Eric took out some pistols from the Police Station. I didn't ask too many questions. He says they're useful in shooting rats and we never know what emergencies we may face.

SUNDAY

Outside the Greyfriar pub. It has wine and beer aplenty. Good Pompey Royal: Strong Bitter. Inside, the pub is dark and smelly. It is dark under the low.

oak beams...
I keep on looking at the red phone box
and think: It will never ring again.

Went inside the Church of St. Nicholas.
I loved the broken stained glass on
the windows and the minton tiles on
the floor of the sanctuary. Then I
went to pull at the ropes of the ancient
bells in the belfry. I pulled for a long
time. All the others came into the
church. Then, silently, we all knelt
and prayed. I guess I prayed for
miracles and for my Will.

A WEDNESDAY

I have less and less desire to write
in the diary. Something tells me
I'm pregnant... a new life. Could
it be healthy?

Eric has been trying to pick up a

radio station somewhere ... but all is silent ...

A Tuesday?

Watched a spider spinning its web off-balance. The web had just a few strands on top and an excess on the bottom half. Poor spider. It must be the effect of radiation. Does it suffer? I wonder if I am spinning my own irregular web?

A Saturday?

I feel increasingly lethargic
No energy. Carol says she feels
just like I do. She looks terrible.
Poor, lovely Carol. She's lost all her
hair. She's taken to weaving a
wig. I agree it's less frightening.

SUNDAY

— if yesterday indeed was a Saturday.
I can't stand writing all these medical
reports. I want to write about this
little village and its beauty and its
past... but I guess Jane Austen did
all of that very well so long, long
ago...

I like looking out of the window at
the Cedar tree as the sun rises... but
it is so sad that there are no birds...

Eric tells me he thinks the ozone layer
has been destroyed, or at least partially
scattered. That is why things are
burning up and it all looks so brown.

A Monday

Drank too much again. There seems
little else to do. We've planted all
the repaired greenhouses with seed
packets... I don't have much faith in
how they'll come out. Were they not
all contaminated?

TUESDAY

Strange, my nightmares have stopped.
I seem more at peace. Is it resignation?
Defeat? Or the approach of a new era?

A Wednesday

Spent a long time wandering about
the graveyard of St. Nicholas, looking
at the generations of knights buried
there. Then came back to the house
and talked to Eric and Carol about
Chaos, the vast, eternal God of dark-
ness of Greek mythology. I remembered

reading about it in <u>Larousse</u>. Eric pointed out that Chaos came from the Greek root, meaning "to gape." Chaos was a pure cosmic principle, like the primordial ocean. Eric explained to us that only later, because of the similarity to the word meaning "to pour" did chaos become identified with confusion and lack of organization of the elements in space. Eric should have been a scholar... the profundity of his knowledge is so wasted on us. I feel so shallow by comparison.

A day... or night.

A gang of youthful marauders came by... so there are people alive after all ... pillagers, as in the days of the Norsemen. They came looking for food. At first they threatened to kill us, but when they saw we were too weak to fight and with no good food, they simply left. They were like a wolf pack : murderous, mean, dirty, with empty minds and horrid lip sores. Better to die than to live like that.

Another day

Carol died yesterday. Eric and I both cried and cried. We both held her hands as she left us. Her last words were : "I'm almost there."
It is so unbelievably, irretrievably sad. I think I loved her very, very much towards the end ... We buried her under a dead boxwood in the churchyard. All the box-woods are dead.   Amen.

An afternoon

Saw a couple of spotted flycatchers.
First birds I have seen since I came
here. I wonder where they're from?

I feel more and more alone.

A morning... much later

Simon, Diana and Ann have
decided to join up and leave. They
don't want to starve waiting for
the vegetables in the hot houses to
ripen. They all have bleeding gums.
Their ankles are swollen. I'm not
sure whether this is from a bad diet
or radiation. They are so young...
but I haven't the strength to talk
them out of it ... Yes, maybe it is
the drink ...

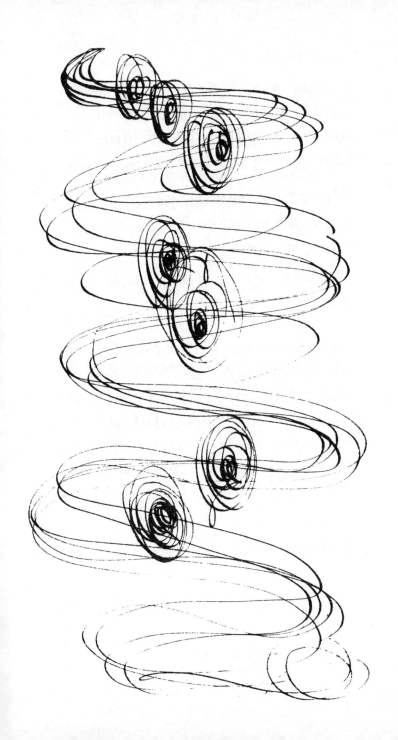

An evening

I do love Eric. There is nothing that keeps us going, keeps us alive, but our love for one another, I think. He is now my only link to any reality.

I looked the other day in the mirror and was frightened. Yes, frightened. I did not recognize HER : ME. Yes, that was _me_. I don't want to face her again.

Whatever happens, and I don't know what will happen, whether Eric and I shall live to see our children ever again. I cannot, I will not make any more entries in this diary. The past is filled with too much horror to remember. I must try again, as in the old days, to live in the present. A minute, an hour, a day at a time.

Jenny

PENGUIN BOOKS

Penguin Books Ltd, Harmondsworth, Middlesex, England
Penguin Books, 625 Madison Avenue, New York, New York 10022, U.S.A.
Penguin Books Australia Ltd, Ringwood, Victoria, Australia
Penguin Books Canada Ltd, 2801 John Street, Markham, Ontario, Canada L3R 1B4
Penguin Books (N.Z.) Ltd, 182-190 Wairau Road, Auckland 10, New Zealand

First published in Great Britain by Centaur Press 1981
Published simultaneously in the U.S.A.
and Canada by Little, Brown and Co. 1982
Published in Penguin Books 1983

Copyright © Yorick Blumenfeld, 1981
All rights reserved

Calligraphy by Gerald Fleuss

Made and printed in Great Britain by
Richard Clay (The Chaucer Press) Ltd,
Bungay, Suffolk